SUNDAY

Synthia Saint James

Albert Whitman & Company · Morton Grove, Illinois

Text and illustrations copyright © 1996
by Synthia Saint James.
Published in 1996 by Albert Whitman & Company,
6340 Oakton Street, Morton Grove, Illinois 60053-2723.
Published simultaneously in Canada by General Publishing,
Limited, Toronto.
Printed in the United States of America.
10 9 8 7 6 5 4 3 2 1

Library of Congress Cataloging-in-Publication Data

Saint James, Synthia.
Sunday / written and illustrated by Synthia Saint James.
        p.   cm.
Summary: Portrays an African American family with twin girls as
they spend a typical Sunday eating breakfast, going to church,
and visiting their grandparents.
ISBN 0-8075-7658-1
1. Afro-Americans—Juvenile fiction. [1. Afro-Americans—Fiction.
2. Family life—Fiction. 3. Twins—Fiction.] I. Title.
PZ7.S1424Su 1996   95-52934

[E]—dc20   CIP   AC

The text typeface is Tekton.
The illustrations are rendered in acrylic on canvas.
The design is by Susan B. Cohn.

For Taiwo, Kehinde,
Trena, Rufus, Guy,
Garrett, and Chisai.

Sunday morning,

sleeping late;

pancakes piled high.

Reading the paper,

dressing in our
Sunday best,

walking together
to church.

1949

Grandma and
Grandpa meet us.

We listen to our preacher's sermon.

Joyful voices sing!

We visit with friends

big and small.

Riding the subway,

listening to stories,

remembering
good times,

helping Grandma
fix supper.

At blessing time,

Dad gives thanks.

Sunday is for family!